D1321192

SHORT!
A Book of Very Short Stories

This is a book of the shortest stories—some familiar, some brand new, and some retold in a different way. There are ghost stories and wonder tales, fables, practical jokes, modern horror stories, and myths. The stories include Anansi the spider man, the ghost on the bridge, people who make the right or wrong choice, animals that talk (of course), and a little voice in a dark room (when there shouldn't be anyone there). Many, many stories. That's enough. Best to keep it short!

Kevin Crossley-Holland is a distinguished teller of tales. He is also a poet, translator, broadcaster, and writer for children, and is a winner of the Carnegie Medal. He specializes in myth, legend, and folk-tales, especially from the Anglo-Saxon period and from East Anglia. He has four children, and lives in Norfolk.

Other books for children from the same author and publisher

Beowulf (illustrated by Charles Keeping)
The Green Children (illustrated by Alan Marks)
The Young Oxford Book of Folk-tales (editor) (forthcoming)

KEVIN CROSSLEY-HOLLAND

SHORT!

A BOOK OF
VERY SHORT STORIES

OXFORD UNIVERSITY PRESS

Oxford University Press, Great Clarendon Street, Oxford OX2 6DP

Oxford New York
Athens Auckland Bangkok Bogota Bombay
Buenos Aires Calcutta Cape Town Dar es Salaam
Delhi Florence Hong Kong Istanbul Karachi
Kuala Lumpur Madras Madrid Melbourne
Mexico City Nairobi Paris Singapore
Taipei Tokyo Toronto

and associated companies in
Berlin Ibadan

Oxford is a trade mark of Oxford University Press

A CIP catalogue record for this book is available
from the British Library

ISBN 0 19 278147 2 (hardback)
ISBN 0 19 278148 0 (paperback)

Inside illustrations by Peter Viccars
Cover illustration by Jon Berkeley

Printed and bound in Great Britain by
Biddles Ltd, Guildford and King's Lynn

for Eleanor and Oenone

Contents

Ghosteses

S IDE BY SIDE, the two men stepped on their spades and dug their allotments until it was time for a tea-break.

'Here! I've been thinking,' one man said.

'Thinking? You?'

The first man sighed and mopped his face. 'You and all your stories,' he said. 'I don't believe in these here ghosteses.'

'You don't?' said the other man.

And he vanished.

Brainless

'WHAT'S WRONG?' asked the woodcutter.
'Look at that,' said his companion.
'That's the spoor of a lion. I don't want to
be eaten by a lion.'

'Come on,' said the woodcutter. 'I'm not going back
home empty-handed. Not after walking all this way.'

'No,' said his companion.

'Well, your wife won't thank you.'

So the woodcutter and his companion quickly
collected all the wood they could carry.

'Time to go home,' said the woodcutter.

'Not by the way we came,' said his companion. 'That
was the spoor of a lion.'

'Then this is where our paths divide,' said the
woodcutter. 'You can take the longer way if you want;
that's up to you.'

So the companion took the longer path up over the
side of the rocky mountain.

Before long, the woodcutter met the lion, who was
sitting plump in the middle of the path.

'Respect, lion!' said the woodcutter.

'Respect, man!' said the lion.

'Well, let me pass, then,' said the woodcutter.

'I'm ill,' said the lion. 'Pretty ill. And what I need is brains—human brains—if I've ever to get well again. That's why God has offered you to me.'

'I see,' said the woodcutter. 'Yes . . . The only trouble is: I have no brains.'

'No brains?'

'That's the trouble, lion. My friends always call me dumb, idiot, brainless . . . '

'Yes, yes,' said the lion.

'I can prove it. If I had any brains, would I have walked along this path after seeing your spoor? The truth is, lion, that the man with brains is somewhere up there on the mountain. He saw your spoor and took the longer path home.'

The lion slowly got to his feet and slowly shook his sick head. 'Respect, man!' he said.

And he began to climb the side of the mountain.

In the Back Seat

ABBY'S MY BEST FRIEND and this happened to her sister, and Abby told me about it, so I know it's true.

Her sister's eighteen and she's got a car, and she's called Rachel. Last week, well, she went to a late night party. Somewhere in town, I don't know where exactly, and it ended very late. About two o'clock.

By the time Rachel drove home, the city was all empty. That's spooky! Anyhow, Rachel got going and she looked in the mirror, and there was this truck kind-of-thing, right behind her. She could see the driver, and he was big and leaning forward and well . . . he started flashing her: headlights, dipped lights, no lights. No lights in the dark, that's really dangerous. Well, the man kept flashing her and Rachel didn't know what to do. She just drove as fast as she could. But when she turned left, the man turned left. Then Rachel turned right into Lake Street, that's where Abby lives, and this man turned right as well. He even followed her into her own driveway.

Rachel just put her hand on the horn and never took it off. In the middle of the night. Her dad woke straight up and he came rushing down to find out what was going on.

'That man!' cried Rachel. 'He's been following me and flashing me right across town.'

Then the driver got out of his truck kind-of-thing. He was big and he had a scar on one cheek—you could see the stitches. 'Quick!' he said. 'There's a man in her back seat. I flashed her every time I saw him raise the axe.'

Then Abby's father yelled and just dragged Rachel out of the car. And the driver with the scar, he ripped open the back door and fell on the man hiding there.

Wrestling

THERE WAS a prince who decided to ask one wild animal to live with him. But which one? The prince scratched his big ears. 'That's up to them,' he said. 'The animals must decide for themselves.'

'Fast food!' yelped raccoon.

'Central heating!' growled polar bear.

'Air conditioning!' roared tiger.

'Soft carpets!' grunted tapir.

'Sweet showers!' whinnied zebra.

All the wild animals wanted to live with the prince.

'But that's impossible,' said lion. 'Only one of us can go and live with him. We had better settle it by wrestling.'

First, elephant wrestled with grunting wild boar and threw him on his back. Then lion wrestled with elephant and threw him on his back. And then the goat wrestled with lion and threw him on his back. So it went on until only two animals were left: hyena and cat.

'No contest!' said hyena. 'I'm a hundred times stronger than you.'

Cat slowly licked her chops. 'Shall we step outside then?' she said.

True, hyena was far stronger than cat. But each time he tossed her in the air, cat fell on her feet and sprang at hyena again.

'I'm the winner,' screamed hyena.

'No, you're not,' said the other animals. 'To win, you have to throw your opponent on her back.'

So hyena tossed cat into the air again, and once more cat landed on her feet. In the end, hyena was so exhausted that he lay down and fell asleep, and rolled over on to his back. Then all the wild animals howled that cat was the winner.

So cat went to live with the prince. She could wander wherever she wanted, and eat whenever she wanted; she could arch her back and rub herself against his shins.

In fact, cat is still there. She still lives with the prince. When he talks to her she sometimes purrs and sometimes stares at him with frosty blue eyes.

'Wild!' says the prince. Then he strokes cat's fur the wrong way, and it crackles and sparks like metal in a microwave.

The Song of the Syrup

'LISTEN CAREFULLY,' said the woman. 'Are you listening? That liquid up there—in the yellow jug—it may be poisonous.'

'Poisonous?'

'Just leave it alone. It could kill you. And if it doesn't, I will.'

But the boy wasn't that stupid; and he thought his mother might be saving the syrup for herself. So as soon as she had gone out, he stood on a chair and reached up for the yellow jug.

Ah! The scent of the syrup sang a sweet song inside the boy's head. So he lifted the jug and opened his mouth and drank it all—except for the bit that trickled down his chin on to his jersey. The boy wiped that away with his wrist.

For a moment he felt as contented and drowsy as a well-fed bee. But soon he began to think. Then he drew in his breath, shook his head, and dropped the jug onto the stone floor. It broke into dozens of bright yellow splinters.

When the woman came back, she found the larder door closed and her son inside the larder, crying his eyes out.

'I'm going to kill you,' she stormed.

'I just wanted to sniff,' said the boy, 'but I dropped your yellow jug, and I knew you'd be so angry I wanted to k . . . k . . . kill myself. So I drank the poison.'

'Go on,' said the woman.

'It didn't work,' said the boy. 'So then I smeared it over my clothes, my hair as well. And it still hasn't w . . . w . . . worked.'

Leopard, Goat, and Yam

'AS SOON AS my master's son leaves me alone with you,' bleated goat to yam, 'I'm going to eat you.'

'And as soon as he leaves me alone with you,' purred leopard to goat, 'I'm going to eat you.'

But the boy heard them and understood them. So when he came to the bank of the grey-green river and saw the little grey-green canoe, and realized that he couldn't ferry over leopard, goat, and yam all at the same time, what did he do?

This is what he did.

First he paddled over goat and yam.

'As soon as my master's son leaves me alone with you,' croaked yam to goat, 'you're going to eat me.'

But the boy took goat back with him across the grey-green river. When he crossed a second time, he took leopard with him. And he paddled back alone.

Then the boy crossed a third time, taking goat with him.

And then, whistling, he went on his way—and leopard, goat, and yam all went with him.

Dead and Alive

OLD MAN stared at his handiwork. 'I have a world,' he said. 'I have man. But something's still missing.'

Then Old Man thought and thought until he knew what. 'Woman,' he said. 'Woman and child are missing.'

For four days Old Man kneaded and moulded a lump of clay. But he didn't like any of his woman-shapes. Not at all. At the end of the fourth day, though, Old Man made a shape he liked very much. 'Mmm!' he murmured. So he made a little child much the same shape as woman.

'Woman and child,' said Old Man. 'Now they need life.' So he put the clay shapes under a cover.

On the first day the shapes twitched, on the second day they raised their heads, on the third they waved their arms and legs, and on the fourth they began to crawl around.

'You are ready,' said Old Man. 'Stand up. Walk on my world.'

Woman and child followed Old Man down to the river, and there he sprinkled each of them with the water of sound.

It didn't take too long for woman to start talking. 'What are we?' she asked. 'I mean, what are we?'

'You are alive,' said Old Man. 'You can walk and dance and breathe.'

'Were we alive when we were pieces of clay?' asked woman.

'No,' said Old Man.

'We weren't? But if we weren't alive, what were we? What are we when we aren't alive?'

'Dead,' said Old Man. 'If you're not alive, you're dead.'

'Will we always be alive?' asked woman. 'Will we live for ever and ever or will we be dead again?'

Old Man looked at woman. 'I never thought of that,' he said. 'But we can settle it here and now. Throw this old cowpat into the water. If it floats, people who die can live again four days later.'

'What if the water dissolves the cowpat?' asked the woman. 'Look!' she said. 'Here's a stone. If it sinks, people will die, but if it floats, they will live for ever.' And with that, woman threw the stone into the water.

The stone sank.

(Well, woman had only been alive for a few minutes, so she still had something left to learn.)

'That's that,' said Old Man. 'What is done cannot be undone. People will have to die.'

Golden Hand

THE MAN loved his wife. He loved her mop of blonde hair. He loved her tawny eyes and warm breath that smelt of peardrops. He loved the way she walked like a penguin. But above all, he loved her solid gold left hand.

Poor woman! She died while she was still quite young, and the man was filled with emptiness. He felt as if he had lost a limb.

On the night after the funeral, the man went back to the graveyard, and he was carrying a spade. He found his wife's grave, and he dug for an hour and dug up his wife. At once, he unscrewed her left hand and took it back home with him. In fact, so as to be completely safe, he hid it under his bottom pillow.

But when the man got into bed, it didn't matter whether he closed his eyes or kept them open: his bedroom still swarmed with dancing white lights, like insects' stings or stars. And little white bones were floating through the air.

Then the man saw his wife—his wife's ghost—drift up to the foot of the bed.

'Where is your mop of hair?' he asked.

'Fallen out,' she said. 'Turned into dust.'

22

'Where are your eyes?'

'Marbled,' she said. 'Marbled and shrivelled.'

'And your breath?'

'Cold,' she said. 'Cold and wormy.' And then she stepped along the side of the bed. The man could have reached out and touched her.

'And your left hand?' he asked. 'Wife, where is your left hand?'

The woman leaned forward and bent down. 'GONE!' she shrieked. 'IT'S GONE! AND YOU'VE GOT IT!'

Ouch!

FIVE SHEPHERDS fell asleep under a tree. And in their sleep they sighed and stretched and tossed and turned and tied their legs into a knot. When they woke up, they didn't know which leg belonged to who.

'I'm hungry,' said one shepherd.

'And I'm thirsty,' said another.

All five of them were thirsty and hungry, but they were unable to stand up.

'What's wrong with you, men?' shouted a woman on her way to the well. 'The sun's up and you're still on your backs.'

'We can't stand up,' said the shepherds. 'We don't know which leg belongs to who.'

'What's it worth?' asked the woman.

'Worth?' said one shepherd. 'Worth? I don't know. How about ten toes of tobacco?'

'Fifty,' said the woman. 'Fifty toes and I'll show you which leg belongs to who.'

'All right,' said the shepherds.

Then the woman unfastened her sun-and-moon brooch, and stuck the pin into the nearest foot.

'Ouch!' yelled one shepherd.

'That's one of yours,' said the woman. 'Pull, man! Pull!'

Then the woman stuck another foot.

'Ouch!'

'That's yours.'

'Ouch!'

'Pull, man! Pull!'

One by one the shepherds stood up on their stiff feet. And each poor man fished in his pocket for ten toes of tobacco.

The Hook

I T WAS THE SAME most evenings. Sam picked up Becky and drove his wreck to the parking area two miles outside town. There they could play the car radio full blast; they could hang out on their own.

It was already half-dark when they heard the local news: ' . . . escaped from Locksley Prison . . . convicted for murder . . .'

Sam stopped drumming his fingers on the tacky steering-wheel.

' . . . a full-scale hunt is under way,' droned the voice on the dashboard. 'Police are advising members of the public not to approach him. He is extremely dangerous, and has a hook instead of a right arm.'

'A hook!' said Becky. 'That's horrible.'

'Horrible, horrible!' said Sam, grinning in the dark.

'What was that?' cried Becky, and she jammed herself against Sam.

'What?'

'That scratching!'

'Keep your shirt on,' said Sam. 'This piece of junk's always creaking and groaning.'

26

'Let's go,' said Becky. 'Now, Sam. Quick!'
'If you insist,' said Sam.

'Sorry,' said Becky, when Sam pulled up outside her house. 'I just got scared. You coming in?'

Then Sam jumped up and walked round the back of the car to Becky's side. And there, hanging from the handle of Becky's door, hanging and still swinging, was a large steel hook.

A Mouthful to Eat

NO JOB; NO MONEY; NO FOOD. One day the poor woman hurt so much she stole a squawking chicken, and wrung its neck, and ran half-way up the mountain with it. There she cleaned it and made a fire; she picked wild herbs; and she popped the chicken into her cooking pot.

The woman was just about to eat when a man came striding down the mountain. 'Just my luck!' she said to herself. 'I have no luck!' And she quickly hid the pot in a scrubby bush.

'What are you doing up here?' asked the man.

'Resting,' said the woman.

'I can smell your chicken and I'm hoping you'll give me a mouthful to eat.'

'No,' said the woman.

'You would if you knew who I was,' said the man.

'Who are you?'

'I am God,' said the man. 'Your Lord.'

'That settles it,' said the woman. 'The way you treat people like me! I have no job; no money; no food. Your favourites have jobs and money and food and houses and gardens and horses and I . . . You're so unfair I'm not even going to give you a mouthful.'

'I'll give you one chance to change your mind,' said God.

'Go away!' said the woman.

So God went striding down the mountain, and the woman pulled her cooking pot out of the bush. She was just about to eat when a second man came down the mountain. He was very thin and very pale.

'Have you got a mouthful for me to eat?' asked the man.

'No,' said the woman.

'You would have if you knew who I was,' said the man.

'Who are you, then?' asked the woman.

'I am Death,' said the man.

'You are?' exclaimed the woman. 'Well! You're always fair. It doesn't matter whether we're thin or fat, female or male, black or white or red or yellow, rich or poor, you take us all, and you have no favourites. Yes, you can have a mouthful of my chicken.'

That's None of Your Business

THAT CLOCK! It was like a piece of icing done by a goddess, dropped out of heaven. It was white as white, and inlaid with little mirrors and misty pearls. The tick-and-tock of it was as close and comforting as the beats of your own heart, and the music it made on the hour, every hour, came straight from paradise.

Every boy and girl in the village came round to listen to it, and look at it. How longingly they looked at it!

So when they grew up and I grew old, and had little time for grand possessions, I thought I might just give it away. 'I'll give it to whoever can mind his—or her—own business for a whole year.' That's what I said.

On the last night of the year, a young man knocked on the door. 'I've minded my own business for a whole year,' he said.

I believed him. He was a dull sort of lad, the kind that never asks questions and doesn't seem too interested in other people or the wonders of the world.

As I went into the back room to fetch the clock, I called out, 'You're the second who's come to claim the clock.'

'The second!' exclaimed the young man. 'Why didn't the first get it?'

'That's none of your business,' I said. 'So *you* won't get the clock.'

I left the clock on the mantelpiece. There it is! Inlaid with little mirrors and misty pearls. It's like a piece of icing done by a goddess, dropped out of heaven.

Slam and the Ghosts

'**Y**OUR BROTHER! I'll brain him! Bursting in at one o'clock night after night! Leaving his great hoof marks all over the house!'

'I'll talk to him,' said Douglas. 'I'll talk to Slam.'

'It's the grog,' said their mother. 'It's wrecking him. Can't you get him off it?'

Secretly, Douglas agreed with his mother. What Slam really needs, he thought, is a bit of a shock.

Half-way between the pub and their house, the lane passed under a very steep bank; and at the top of the bank was the old disused graveyard.

That same night, very late, Douglas pulled the white sheet off his bed. He let himself quietly out of the house and, under stars sharp as thorns, walked up to the graveyard right on top of the bank, overlooking the lane.

'This will cure him,' Douglas said to himself. 'Kill him or cure him. Poor old Slam!'

Before long, Slam came staggering up the lane. His shoes were made of lead, and he was singing a wordless song. When his brother was right beneath him, Douglas stood up and whoo-hooed at him.

'I know,' said Slam, and he added a great hiccup. 'You're the ghost! I know!'

Douglas whoo-hooed again and Slam peered up at the graveyard and tottered sideways.

'Two ghosts!' exclaimed Slam. 'There was only one ghost last night.'

Slowly Douglas turned round, and stared straight into two furious, glaring eyes. Douglas started back and fell head first over the steep bank. He landed at his brother's feet and broke his neck. Poor old Douglas! That was the end of him.

Butterflies

THE GIRL SAT on the sofa with her homework book on her knee. 'Butterfly Poem' she wrote at the top of the page. She could hear the thump thump-a-thump of the pop music in the flat upstairs. Then a boy shoved the evening newspaper through the letter-box—and then the telephone rang . . .

How difficult it was to concentrate.

But after a while the girl caught a few colourful words and set them down on her white page. Then some more. And the more words she caught, the easier they became to catch, the best words in the world.

Next morning, the girl got ready to go to school. She opened her homework book and flicked to the page headed 'Butterfly Poem'. But where were the words? They had all gone. The girl looked at her book in amazement—she turned it upside down, she checked no page had been torn out, she leafed through it in case the words had somehow escaped to another page . . .

Then it seemed to the girl as if her arms and legs were made of air, and her head was rising through the ceiling. She kissed her mum goodbye and closed the front door . . .

The girl rubbed her eyes. She screwed them up and opened them again. All around her were little scraps of orange and turquoise and jasmine and violet: the whole grey street where she lived was quick and brightly-coloured with hundreds and thousands of butterflies.

Tit For Tat

'THERE'S A DECENT PLACE to eat on the other side of the river,' jackal told camel. 'The field of sugar cane will suit you. And the crabs and little bits of fish on the river-bank will suit me.'

So camel swam across the river; and jackal, who didn't know how to swim, sat on camel's back.

Then jackal ran up and down the river-bank, snapping at all the crab and little bits of fish, and he ate so fast that he finished before camel had chewed more than a couple of mouthfuls of sugar cane. Then jackal hurried up to the sugar cane field, and ran right round it, yelping and howling.

'That good for nothing!' said the villagers. 'Scratching holes! Wrecking the sugar cane roots! Let's chase that jackal away.'

When they reached the field, the villagers were surprised to see not only a jackal but a hungry camel. They shouted and beat the camel and chased him all the way back to the river-bank.

'Time to go home,' said jackal.

'Jump on my back,' said camel.

Then camel waded across the shallows into deep water, and started to swim.

'What in the world were you doing, yelping and howling like that?' camel asked. 'Everyone in the village heard you. I've been shouted at and beaten, and I haven't even had a decent meal.'

'It's how I am, camel,' jackal said. 'When I've eaten, I need to sing.'

'I see,' said camel. And he kept swimming until they were right in the middle of the river. 'Jackal,' said camel. 'I need to roll over.'

'No,' said jackal. 'Why do you need to roll over?'

'It's how I am, jackal,' camel said. 'After a good supper, I need to roll over.'

Then camel rolled over in the water. Jackal was swept away, and camel bared his yellow teeth and swam back home.

Poor Vera

POOR VERA died while Louise was gently stroking her left paw. First Louise cried, and then she decided Vera should at least have a decent funeral.

'I can't bury her here,' Louise told her friend Emily on the telephone. 'You know what our yard's like.'

'All concrete,' said Emily.

'And all her claws were pulled out before we got her,' wailed Louise, 'and she couldn't climb trees, and she was afraid to go outdoors . . .'

'Bring her round ours,' said Emily. 'We'll pick some flowers and put her at the end of the garden.'

So before her mother or father got home, Louise set off to meet Emily at the supermarket, carrying a plastic bag with Vera inside it, lightly covered with tissue paper.

'Let's have a look,' said Emily.

'Later,' said Louise.

'We can get an ice-cream, anyhow,' said Emily. 'I've got some money, Lou.'

Louise carefully put down the plastic bag on an empty rack next to the cereals, and the two girls headed across the store to the freezer.

'What about KitKats, then?' said Emily. 'In memory of Vera.'

While they were still trying to make up their minds, Louise and Emily heard a shout, and watched as several people gathered and bent down beside one of the check-out counters.

'What's happened?' asked Louise.

Then they saw. On the stone floor lay a big woman, very big, spread-eagled like a starfish. Beside her were a couple of spilled plastic bags. And there was a third bag lying right across her bosom: poor Vera's head was sticking out of it.

The Most Beautiful Sound

APOET invited three musicians to his house for
supper.

'You musicians,' he said, 'you're always
squabbling, you never agree on a single thing.'

'We do,' said one musician.

'No, we don't,' said the second.

'Poets are worse,' said the third.

'Tell me, then,' said the poet. 'What is the most
beautiful sound? Can you agree on that?'

'The nerve of the violin,' said the violinist.

'The bugle of bravery,' said the bugler.

'The heart's drum,' said the drummer.

'What did I tell you?' said the poet.

The musicians were very hungry. They were very
thirsty. But the poet offered his guests nothing to eat and
nothing to drink. Nothing at all.

'I'm ravenous,' said one musician.

'I'm so thirsty,' said the second.

'I could eat my own instrument,' said the third.

At midnight, the poet went out into the kitchen and
returned with a huge casserole full of the most delicious
stew. The very smell of it made the three musicians mad
with hunger.

The poet lifted the lid of the casserole and began to tap it with a large steel spoon. Clink! Clink–clink! Then he banged the lid down on to the casserole again. Clank!

'The song of the cooking pot!' said the poet. 'The music of food! When you're starving, that's the most beautiful sound of all.'

The Mirror

THEY DID HAVE OTHER THINGS. They had sky-dragons. They had pale porcelain bowls that sang with piping blue voices. They had clicking ivory characters and bearded calligraphers. But in that far-off village and far-off time, they had no mirrors. No mirrors at all! Most people had never even heard of them.

The young farmer had heard about mirrors, though, and he wanted to give one to his young bride, so she could see what others saw: the crescents of her eyebrows; her yellow-black and misty eyes. So the young man sold one of his three cows, and he walked for three days to the great city, and used almost all the money to buy a mirror.

Moonrise and sunset: in giving birth to her first child —a daughter—the young wife died. Then her husband could not bear even to look at the mirror. He hid it away at the bottom of an old trunk.

As she grew up, his daughter sometimes asked people about her mother. 'You are beautiful in the same strange way she was,' they told her. 'The same eyebrows. And the eyes. Here! The little crease in the corner of your mouth.'

Fifteen, sixteen . . . One day, when the girl was seventeen, she started rooting around in the attic, looking for something different to wear. But what she found, at the bottom of the old trunk, was her mother's mirror.

The girl looked into it. She looked and then she ran down to her father. 'I've found her,' she cried. 'She's still here. You should have told me. Look!'

But the father did not look; and his love and pain were so great that at first he could not cry. Sunset and moonrise. The man held his shining daughter in his arms.

Mare's Eggs

WHEN HE SAW THE MARROW, Kevin's eyes brightened. There it lay, swollen and striped, amongst all the carrots and onions and potatoes and radishes, and he had never seen anything like it before.

'No day's a good day unless you learn something new,' Kevin said to himself. So he stepped into the shop and asked the greengrocer to tell him what the strange object was.

'That,' said the greengrocer, 'that is a mare's egg.'

'A mare's egg,' cried Kevin. 'Can I buy it?'

'It's yours for one pound,' said the greengrocer.

So Kevin bought the marrow and, to while away the time on his way back home across the heath, he tried to see how far ahead of him he could roll it. Before long, the marrow ran into a bush and a hare leaped out of the bush and galloped away as fast as his legs could carry him.

Then Kevin gave chase. But long-legged as he was, he wasn't as quick as the leaping hare, and the animal escaped him.

Next day, Kevin walked into town again and went back to the greengrocer's shop.

'You again,' said the greengrocer warily. 'Well! What can I do for you today?'

'That was a racehorse's egg,' said Kevin.

'Is that right?' said the greengrocer, grinning.

'It broke and the foal galloped away from me. I couldn't catch up with it.'

'Really?' said the greengrocer.

'So,' said Kevin, 'have you got any carthorse's eggs?'

Room for One More

HOW DIFFICULT it was to sleep in that strange bed! She wrestled with the duvet and thumped the pillow; she turned her back on the flimsy curtains; she wished she had never come up to London.

At midnight she heard the grandfather clock whirr and strike; and then she heard the gravel in the driveway crunch. At once she jumped out of bed and crossed the room and just peeped between the curtains.

What she could see was a gleaming black hearse. But there was no coffin in it, and no flowers. No, the hearse was packed out with living people: a crush of talking, laughing, living people.

Then the driver of the hearse looked straight up at her, as she peeped between the curtains.

'There's room for one more.' That's what he said. She could hear his voice quite clearly. Then she tugged the curtains so they crossed over, and ran back across the room, and jumped into bed, and pulled the duvet up over her head. And when she woke up next morning, she really wasn't sure whether it was all a dream or not.

That day, she went shopping. In the big store, she did Levis Jeanswear on the fifth floor; she did Adidas

Sportswear and that was on the sixth floor; and then she did cosmetics and that was on the seventh floor. Carrying two bags in each hand, she walked over to the lift. But when the bell pinged and the doors opened, she saw the lift was already jammed full with people.

The lift attendant looked straight at her as she stood there with her bags. 'There's room for one more,' he said. And his face was the face of the driver of the hearse.

'No,' she said quickly. 'No, I'll walk down.'

Then the lift door closed with a clang. At once there was a kind of grating screech, and a terrible rattling, then a huge double thud.

The lift in the big store dropped from top to bottom of the shaft, and every single person in it was killed.

A Bit of Commonsense

'I'M GOING TO GET RICH QUICK,' Anansi the spiderman said to himself. 'I'm going to collect all the commonsense in the world. Then people will have to come to me for advice, and I'll charge them for it.'

So whenever Anansi heard anything sensible, he went straight home and whispered the words into the mouth of his calabash. And when a year had gone by, he decided to hide the calabash at the top of a tall tree.

Anansi twisted a rope round the neck of the calabash and tied the two loose ends at the back of his own neck, so that the calabash swung in front of him, and then he started to climb the tree. It was very slow going, though, because the calabash kept bumping him and getting in his way.

Then Anansi heard a scuffling and a laughing far below; and when he peered down, over the rim of the calabash, he saw two boys.

'That man's completely stupid,' one of them said. 'If you're climbing frontways, you put the calabash on your back.'

'He's got no sense at all,' said the second boy.

Anansi was so angry he pulled the rope over his head

and dropped the calabash. It bounced from branch to branch, and then it smashed on the ground.

At once the two boys ran away. And all the commonsense in the calabash blew away. It blew north and south, east and west, to your house and to mine. Everyone got a bit of it. You did. I did. We all did.

Three Questions

'MIKE HASN'T SAID GOOD NIGHT,' Ellie
wailed after her mother. 'He hasn't said good
night to me.'

Two minutes later, Mike invaded his little sister's
bedroom. 'You still owe me,' he said.

'I know,' said Ellie.

'Well?'

'I haven't got it yet.'

'Tell you what,' said Mike, 'I'll let you off if you can
answer three questions.'

'What questions?' asked Ellie in a flat voice. Horrible
hard fraction questions, nasty spelling questions: she
knew she wouldn't be able to answer them.

'One, what can you keep even when you give
it to someone else?' asked Mike. 'Two, how many
stars are there in the sky? And three, what am I
thinking?'

'I know the first,' said Ellie. 'My promise.'

'Who told you that?'

'Harriet! What was the second one?'

'Stars,' said Mike.

'Wait a minute,' said Ellie. She got out of bed, and
walked across to the window, and peered between the

curtains. 'I remember now,' she said. 'Nine hundred and ninety-nine.'

'Says who?'

'There are,' protested Ellie.

'How do you know?'

'If you don't believe me,' said Ellie, 'you can count them for yourself.'

'Huh!' said Mike. 'All right, what am I thinking?'

'Not fair,' said Ellie. 'That's like saying, "What's in my pocket?"'

'Do you give up?'

Ellie pressed her nose into the window; then she had an idea; and then she saw herself begin to smile. 'Mi-ike,' she began slowly, 'you think you're talking to Ellie.'

'What do you mean?'

'What I said.'

'Of course I am,' said Mike.

'I'm not Ellie at all. Mum just told me. They called me Rosie when I was born. When I was christened. But when I stayed pale and sort-of thin—when I wasn't rosy, they changed my name.'

'Are you making that up?' asked Mike.

'So . . . you let me off?' asked Ellie.

Do You Think I Was Born Yesterday?

'I'M SO HUNGRY,' said camel.
'I could eat a tasty tourist,' said wolf.
'Or even a tough traveller,' said fox.

The three friends sniffed around, but all they could find was one stale loaf of bread.

'It's too small to share,' said camel.

'Then who is going to eat it?' asked wolf.

'The oldest,' said fox. 'That's fair, isn't it?'

'That's me, then,' said wolf. 'I am wolf. I went into the Ark with Noah.'

'Really?' said fox. 'Then that makes you much the same age as my grandson. When God created Adam and Eve and all the beasts of the field, I'm the very creature He named fox.'

Then fox and wolf saw that camel had already lifted the loaf high above their heads, and was happily munching it.

Camel looked down his nose. 'For such small creatures, you have ceratainly got a lot to say for yourselves,' he said, and he was talking with his mouth full. 'Noah, indeed! Adam and Eve! How long do you think it took me to grow these long legs? Do you think I was born yesterday?'

Fox and wolf raced round and round camel, but there was no way they could stop him eating or harm him.

Then camel swallowed the bread. He sucked his teeth and 'Harrumph!', he cleared his throat.

Charger

'I'LL HAVE TO SELL OLD CHARGER,' said the farmer.

'Charger!' exclaimed his wife.

'He's one too many,' the farmer said.

So the farmer set off for the autumn Horse Fair. He rode Charger up the windswept dale, feeling rather glum at the prospect of losing his loyal horse, and weary at the thought of having to walk ten miles to get home again from the Fair.

In the high hills, the farmer met a pedlar, a small little man with a wrinkled face, dressed from top to toe in chestnut brown. He was struggling through the wind and rain, carrying a battered old suitcase.

'You wouldn't sell your horse?' the little man asked.

'That's just what I'm going to do,' replied the farmer.

'How much?'

The farmer narrowed his eyes. 'You could have him for eight pounds,' he said.

'Not eight,' said the little man. 'I'll give you six.' And he dropped a hand into one pocket.

'Seven,' said the farmer.

'Seven it is,' said the little man.

Well now, thought the farmer. Which is better? Seven

pounds for Charger here and now, or eight at the Fair—eight or maybe seven. Or even six?

The farmer looked at the poor wet little man. Then he thought of the long walk home. 'It's a deal,' he said.

With that, the farmer dismounted and the man counted the coins into his hand. 'One, two, three, four, five, six, seven.'

'That's it,' said the farmer.

Then the little man picked up his battered suitcase. He raised one foot as high as his hip, wedged it into a stirrup and swung up into the saddle.

And there and then, right in front of the round-eyed farmer, the little man and Charger sank into the earth.

Boo!

S HE DIDN'T LIKE IT at all when her father had
to go down to London and, for the first time, she
had to sleep alone in the old house.

She went up to her bedroom early. She turned the
key and locked the door. She latched the windows and
drew the curtains. She peered inside her wardrobe, and
pulled open the bottom drawer of her chest-of-drawers;
she got down on her knees and looked under the bed.

She undressed; she put on her nightdress.

She pulled back the heavy linen cover and climbed
into bed. Not to read but to try and sleep—she wanted
to sleep as soon as she could. She reached out and turned
off the lamp.

'That's good,' said a little voice. 'Now we're safely
locked in for the night.'

Children of the Tree

'LEAVE ME ALONE!' said the blossoming tree.
But the woman took no notice.

'Why are you hurting me?' asked the tree. 'You humans care for nothing but yourselves.'

'I am poor,' cried the woman. 'My husband has left me; I have no relatives. I'm cutting you down for firewood, and I'll sell the firewood so I can buy food.'

'I will give you some children,' said the tree. 'They will help you and love you. But you must never lose your temper with them, or lay a hand on them.'

Then the tree turned her own blossoms into bright children, and they all trooped back through the bush to the woman's village.

How blessed that woman was. One girl pounded flour; another cut vegetables; another cooked; and another carried water from the well. One boy ploughed; one hunted; one fished; and one hauled some logs. The woman didn't have to work at all.

But there was one little child who was nothing like as strong as all the others. She was small and slight, and had a twisted foot.

'Our sister shouldn't have to work,' the other children

58

said. 'When she asks for food, feed her. Don't be impatient with her.'

'Whatever you say,' said the woman.

But one day, when the little girl asked for food, the woman lost her temper. 'You do nothing but sit by the fire and whine, whine, whine!' she shouted. 'You bush children, I'm fed up with you all. Get the food out of the pot for yourself.'

Then the little girl cried, not because she was hungry but because the woman had lost her temper. And when her sisters and brothers came home, she told them what the woman had said.

'Bush children, are we?' said the children. 'In that case we'll go back to our bush mother.'

'I didn't mean it,' said the woman.

'You heard what our mother said,' replied the children.

No matter how much the woman begged, it made no difference. All the children trooped back to their mother tree and she turned them into blossoms again.

And the woman: she became poor. As poor and hungry as she had been before.

Who's Who?

JACK WAS FIRST to leave the Hallowe'en party. 'My mum,' he said. 'She wants me back by nine o'clock.'

As soon as he reached the bridge by the river, Jack delved into his bag and brought out the white sheet. Then he hoicked himself up on to the wall, and draped the sheet over him. Just a window for his eyes and nose and mouth: that's all.

This'll teach them, thought Jack. Serve them right for believing in ghosts.

It grew dark. And when clouds drowned the moon, it grew even darker. Jack could hear the gurgling-and-sucking of the river.

They won't be long now, he thought. They'll be coming soon. The party will be over by now.

When Jack turned round, he saw another white shape drifting over the bridge towards him. Drifting, and then she sat down on the wall right next to him.

'You've come to frit your friends,' she said, 'and I've come to frit. We'll both frit together.' Then she moved nearer to him.

Jack pressed on the heels of his hands and edged away from her.

'We'll both frit together,' she said, and she moved even nearer to him.

Again Jack edged away from her.

'Won't we, Jack?' she said, and she reached right out to give him a nudge.

'Don't!' cried Jack. And he raised both arms, lost his balance, and fell head first into the river.

Frost, Sun, and Wind

SOON AFTER she stepped out of doors, the girl came across Frost, Sun, and Wind heading out of the village.

'Good morning!' she said, and she hurried down the lane towards the village school.

'That girl we met,' said Frost after a while. 'Who was she talking to?'

'Me, of course,' said Sun. 'She knows I could burn her.'

'She was talking to me,' said Frost. 'She knows I could cut her.'

'Bah!' blew Wind. 'She was talking to me.'

As Frost, Sun, and Wind were unable to agree, they turned round and ran back into the village and caught up with the girl just before she reached the school.

'Who were you talking to?' they asked her.

'You, Wind,' said the girl.

Then Sun grew very hot. 'In that case,' he said, 'I'll heat you, I'll fry you.'

'Pish!' whispered Wind in the girl's ear. 'I'll puff my cheeks, and purse my lips, and wash you with a cool breeze.'

Then Frost turned extremely cold. 'In that case,' he said, 'I'll freeze your blood, I'll turn you into an ice-girl.'

'Tosh!' whispered Wind in the girl's ear. 'Frost is here today and gone tomorrow. He melts as soon as I puff my cheeks, and purse my lips, and blow.'

Poll

NOT SO LONG AGO a Welsh miner was walking slowly along the shady lane that led out of his village and over to the pit. Countless commas and colons of sunlight were dancing a jig on the road; a little wind sighed in the lime trees. And listening to it, the miner sighed too. The last place he wanted to go on such a day was down to the dark and dusty coalface.

'Good morning!' said a voice.

The miner looked to left. He looked to right. He looked behind him. There was nobody there.

'Good morning!' said the same voice.

Again the miner looked to either side, and in front of him, and behind him. Nobody at all.

Then the miner heard the voice for the third time, and it came from right above his head. Sitting on a gently-swinging branch was a green bird.

For a while the miner stared at it and frowned. Most unusual, he thought. Extremely unusual.

Then the bird opened its beak again. 'Good morning!' it said.

The miner, who was as polite as ever a man was, doffed his cap.

'Beg pardon, sir,' he said. 'I thought you was a bird!'

On the Chopping-Block

IT WAS A CRACKLING AFTERNOON at the end of the autumn, and the man decided to chop some wood. But when he went to his garden shed, his axe was missing.

It's that little beast next door, he thought. He's nicked it. To hack off the leg of the dining table! To whack his sister into pieces! He looks like a thief. Little thug! What's the world coming to? You can't even trust your own neighbours!

Then the man stumped over to the stack of logs at the back of his garage and that is where he found his missing axe.

'Huh!' said the man. 'I must have left it here.'

The man set up his chopping-block and began chopping wood. A few minutes later, the school bus drew up on the road outside. Out stepped his neighbours' daughter, and then their son, and they both waved to him.

Pretty normal, thought the man. They look all right. All right as kids go.

Home from the Sea

ON SATURDAY MORNING, Jack went
down to the creek. To do a bit of crabbing. To
nose around in the flotsam and jetsam, and see
what the tide had thrown up.

'You keep away from the edge!' said his mum. 'Right
away! As if I hadn't got enough to worry about. No
money! No food!'

When he rounded the corner of the Maltings, Jack
saw a man sitting at one end of the jetty. That's where
the little fishing-boats tied up and unloaded their
lobsters and flip–flapping shiners. Well, where they used
to tie up! Jack's father had been the last fisherman in
those parts, but now he was drowned and food for fishes.

'Morning!' said Jack.

But the man did not reply. He didn't even look up.

'Morning!' Jack said again. Then the man did look up.
He had strings of seaweed and pieces of scruff and straw
tangled up in his beard and hair. And he was wearing
thigh boots and an old jersey the sea had starched and
decorated with wavy patterns. Jack looked at the man's
face and hands. They were white and bloated—like
overcooked potatoes. In fact, they looked as if they'd
burst if you poked them.

Jack gripped his crabbing-stick and pail, and took half-a-step backwards. Then he took another. And then he turned and walked away as quickly as he dared. But when he went back round the corner of the Maltings, the sea-man was already waiting for him there. Jack could scarcely breathe. 'Excuse me!' he said loudly, much more loudly than he meant to. And then he did run.

Jack ran up the slip road and right back home. But at his own gate the sea-man was waiting for him. And he nodded—a sort-of no-nonsense, come-here, do-this, follow-me nod that Jack suddenly remembered and recognized.

Then the man strode straight to the garden shed. He pointed to the darkest corner, and Jack began to turn over the flower pots, rusty tins, coils of rope, and string.

Then Jack saw three gold coins, three shiners in the gloom.

'Dad!' cried Jack. 'Oh, Dad!' And he reached out . . .

First his father smiled that smile-round-the-corner of his. Then he began to fade, fade . . . He faded and Jack's eyes stung with hot tears.

The Scales of Justice

KING SHIBI made a promise. He promised to feed and protect each and every creature living in his kingdom.

'Kings shouldn't make promises they can't keep,' said Indra, king of the gods. Then he turned himself into a hawk, and turned the goddess Do Right into a dove, and he chased the dove all over the sky.

Do Right was so afraid that she fluttered down on to King Shibi's lap.

'Give me that dove!' demanded the hawk.

'She has asked me to protect her,' said the king.

'Give me that dove,' repeated the hawk, 'otherwise I'll starve and die.'

'I'll give you other flesh to eat,' said the king.

'Give me your own,' said the hawk.

So that is what the king did. He sliced off pieces of his own flesh, and put them in the scales to balance the weight of Do Right, the dove.

But the more of his own flesh that the king put on the scales, the more heavy the dove became. So then the king knew what he had to do. To balance the weight of Do Right, he had to lay his whole body on the scales.

At once King Shibi heard a voice from heaven. 'You have given your whole self. No one can give more.'

Then the hawk and the dove sang for joy. They turned themselves back into Indra and Do Right. They healed King Shibi and flew away to heaven.

To Each Her Own Foot

MOUSE WAS WALKING through the tall grass, squeaking a little song to herself, when she came across elephant.

'Good morning!' said mouse.

'For you, maybe,' said elephant.

'What's wrong?' asked mouse.

'My back,' said elephant. 'I've ripped it open. I've torn my hide on a pointed branch.' Elephant got down on his front knees and groaned. 'Can you see?' he asked. 'It's deep, isn't it? It feels at least two feet long.'

'It does look quite deep,' said mouse. 'And yes, elephant, it's almost two feet long.'

Then elephant groaned more loudly, and the long grass shook and trembled.

'Mind you,' said mouse, 'that pointed branch: it could never have stabbed you in the heart, could it? You listen to me. Last night, a wild cat chased me. Ow! It almost caught me. Look! With one claw it ripped my side open.'

Elephant looked at mouse rather mistily.

'You see?' squeaked mouse. 'A great gash, right under my heart. It's at least two feet long.'

'Two feet,' snorted elephant. 'From your nose to your tail, you're not one foot long.'

72

'That's unfair,' said mouse.

'Not even half a foot,' said elephant.

'To each her own foot,' squeaked mouse. 'You use your foot to measure your wound; and I'll use my foot to measure mine.'

Talk About Short

HE WAS ALONE, and in the dark; and when
he reached out for the matches, the matches
were put into his hand.

Tommy and the Ghost

'ARE YOU SURE you'll be all right?' asked the owner of the haunted house.

'I know what to do,' said Tommy. 'You just leave me to it.'

'Well, make yourself at home!' said the owner.

That's what Tommy did. As soon as the owner had gone, he stretched out in front of the fire, and finished off the owner's bottle of best brandy.

Just on midnight—the clock in the hall was still striking—there was a kind of rustle. And there was the ghost! Standing right in front of Tommy.

'Hello!' the ghost whispered.

'Hello to you!' said Tommy.

'Well, Tommy, how are you doing?'

'I can't complain,' said Tommy. 'But how do you know my name?'

'Easy,' whispered the ghost. 'I know names.'

'How did you get in here?' Tommy asked. 'Not through that door. I was watching.'

'Through the keyhole.'

'Stuff!' said Tommy. 'I don't believe you.'

'But I did,' whispered the ghost.

'Nonsense!' said Tommy. 'You're too large by half.

76

What next? I suppose you'll tell me you can get through the neck of a bottle?'

'I can and all,' whispered the ghost.

'Never,' said Tommy.

'I can then.'

'Prove it!'

'Look,' whispered the ghost. 'Can't you believe your own eyes, Tommy?'

And with that, the ghost drew itself up, and then drew itself down into the brandy bottle.

At once Tommy put the cork back into the top of the bottle. He went straight out of the house and down to the river and threw the bottle, plunk, under the middle arch.

'You drank all my best brandy!' exclaimed the owner of the house.

'Fair exchange,' said Tommy. 'This house of yours will never be haunted again.'

The Fox and the Geese

A FOX once came across a gaggle of well-fed geese sitting in a meadow. He laughed and said, 'Aha! I've come in the nick of time. You're grouped very nicely so that I can eat you one after the other.'

The geese cackled in terror; they jumped up and began to moan and miserably to beg for their lives.

But the fox would not hear of it, and said, 'No! I won't have mercy. You must die.'

At last one goose summoned up her courage and said, 'If we poor geese must really sacrifice our innocent young lives, grant us just one wish: allow us one last prayer, so we will not die in a state of sin. After that, we promise to stand in a row so that you can take your pick—the fat, the fatter, and the fattest.'

'All right,' said the fox. 'That is fair enough, and it's a pious request: you pray, and for as long as you pray, I'll wait.'

So the first goose began a good long prayer, cackling 'Ga! Ga!' over and over again, and because she showed no sign of coming to an end, the second one did not wait until it was her turn but also began to cackle 'Ga! Ga!'

The third and fourth followed her, and soon they were all cackling together.

(And had they finished their prayers, there would be more to say, but they are still praying and praying, morning, noon, and night.)

Threescore Years and Ten

NOT LONG AFTER God created the world, he measured out the length of each creature's life.

'How long will I live?' ass asked God.

'Thirty years,' said God. 'How does that suit you?'

'Thirty years,' replied ass. 'It makes me tired even to think of it. Thirty years carrying loads. More kicks than compliments. Does it have to be so long?'

God felt sorry when he heard ass, so he took away eighteen years.

'You, dog,' said God. 'How long would you like to live? Will thirty years suit you?'

'Thirty years!' exclaimed dog. 'My paw-pads will wear out. I'll lose my voice, and lose my teeth. And then what? I'll just hobble from corner to corner and growl.'

God felt sorry when he heard dog, so he took away twelve years.

'As for you,' God said to monkey, 'you'll be happy with thirty years, won't you?'

'Do you know why I jibber and jabber?' said monkey. 'To stop myself from crying. How would you like to have to make people laugh—all the time? How would you like to be rewarded with sour apples?'

God felt sorry when he heard monkey, so he took away ten years.

'How long will we live?' woman and man asked God.

'Thirty years,' said God. 'That's long enough, isn't it?'

'Thirty years,' cried woman and man. 'No sooner than we've built our own house and sat at our own hearth; no sooner than we've planted trees and seen them bear fruit, it will be time for us to die. Let us live a little longer.'

'I will give you ass's eighteen years as well,' said God.

'That's not long enough,' said woman and man.

'Ass's eighteen years and dog's twelve years, then.'

'Longer,' said woman and man. 'Please.'

'Well!' said God. 'I'll give you monkey's ten years too. But that's all you can have.'

So woman and man live for seventy years—threescore years and ten. First they live for thirty human years, when they work hard and play hard, and are healthy, and laugh, and love their lives. Then they live ass's eighteen years, when they stagger from one duty to another, and get few thanks for it; then come dog's twelve years when woman and man lie in the corner, and have no teeth, and growl. Then woman and man live monkey's ten years: what they do is stupid, what they say is stupid, and children laugh at them.

Ask the Driver

I T WAS LATE at night when John rolled home with his donkey cart.

First he sang to the stars; then he swallowed his hiccups. 'We'll have to watch out when we get near the crossroads,' John told his donkey. 'That poor pint of a policeman has nothing better to do than spy on people like us, and you know the rules . . .'

'Eeyore,' said the donkey.

'A sight on your dart as poon as it's lark.'

'Sorry?' said the donkey.

'A blight on your tart as moon as it's park.'

'And a third time,' said the donkey.

'A light on your cart . . .'

'That's it,' said the donkey.

'A light on your cart as soon as it's dark,' said John. 'You have to have a light.'

So when they got near the crossroads, John scrambled out of the cart and untied his donkey from the shafts. First he tied the donkey behind the cart so that he could drive it, then he backed himself into the shafts and started to pull the creaking cart up the lane.

Sure enough, the policeman was waiting at the

crossroads. 'John!' he called out. 'Where's your light? You know the rules, John.'

'Blast the diver!' said John.

'What's that?'

'Mask the fiver!' said John.

'And a third time,' brayed the donkey.

'Ask the driver!' said John. 'Ask the driver!'

'Eeyore!' said the donkey.

Talk About Sharp

'KING CHARLES the First walked and talked half an hour after his head was cut off,' my daughter said. 'How can that be?'

'I think I've heard that before,' I said. 'Let me tell you a story while I'm remembering.'

'What story?'

'There was once a whole crew of bandits who were sentenced to death. To be beheaded.'

'Ugh!'

'One of the bandits recognized a soldier who was the owner of a particularly sharp sword. Sharp as a razor.

'"I've heard your sword's so sharp you can cut off a man's head with a single stroke," the bandit said to this soldier.

'"Uh huh!"

'"Would you . . . er . . ."

'"Got you!" said the soldier. "Just stick close by me when we all go out on the killing ground."

'So that's what the bandit did. And out there the soldier unsheathed his sword, and flashed it, and sliced off the bandit's head with one stroke.

'The head rolled away over the dusty ground. And while it was still rolling, the soldier heard it exclaim, "Whew! Talk about sharp!"'

My daughter screwed up her face. Then she cleared her throat. 'Right!' she said. 'What about Charles the First?'

'I can't remember,' I replied.

'King Charles the First walked and talked,' she said. 'Full stop. Half an hour after, his head was cut off.'

The Lion's Den

THE KING of the animals called a meeting in his den. 'Order!' he shouted. 'Order!'

Then all the trumpeting and baying and croaking and barking and hissing and laughing and whistling subsided.

'That's quite enough of that,' said lion. 'Right! First item on the agenda. Does my den smell?'

'Smell?' said skunk.

'Everything smells,' said owl.

'How does it smell?' said lion. 'How does it smell?'

'To tell you the truth, lion,' said dog, 'and not to beat about the bush, to come straight to the point of the matter . . .'

'Get on with it!' said lion.

'Not too good, lion,' said dog. 'In fact, it smells something terrible.'

'How dare you?' roared lion. And he tore the honest dog to pieces. Then the king of the animals glared at all the creatures in his den. 'All right,' he growled, 'how does my den smell?'

'Like mango blossom,' said monkey. 'Your den, it smells like a dream of paradise.'

'You liar!' roared lion. 'You deserve the same fate as dog.' And he tore monkey to pieces.

'What about you, fox?' asked lion. 'How does my den smell?'

'Ah!' said fox, and he sniffed. 'If only I could tell,' he said, and he sneezed. Atishoo! 'If only I could get rid of this dreadful cold!'

Gran's Last Journey

G RAN LOVED SWITZERLAND. She loved
the little rackety mountain trains, the muesli
and spit-and-polish, and the mountains with
icing on them that turned pink in the evening sunlight.

'But what I love most about travelling,' said Gran, 'is
the way things never turn out quite as you expect.'

Gran had been to a mountain village in Switzerland
for her honeymoon and, ten years later, she somehow
raised enough money to take her daughter there.

'How did you do that?' her daughter asked her, when
she was grown up. 'Where did the money come from?'

'I sold my engagement ring,' said Gran.

'You didn't.'

'Dad agreed. One ring's enough for anybody.'

So when Gran was seventy-nine, there was a lot of
talk around the kitchen table. And in the end, Gran's
daughter and her husband and their two children decided
to club together for Gran's eightieth birthday. They
decided to drive across France and get Gran out to
Switzerland one more time.

What a holiday they had! Picnics; walks through
springy, sweet-smelling pinewoods; paddling through
streams so icy cold the water grabbed your ankles; little

expeditions up and down the village street; meals by candlelight.

'The best holiday of all,' said Gran on their last evening. 'You know, I really could stay here for ever.'

And that night, without any fuss, Gran died in her sleep. She just sighed, and let out all her breath, and didn't breathe in again.

'In this place of all places,' said her daughter, crying and smiling.

'Look! We don't want to get caught up with the authorities,' said her husband. 'Gran would hate that. Let's just wrap her up and strap her to the roof-rack and get her home.'

And that's what the family decided to do. They packed their cases, wrapped up Gran, strapped her to the roof-rack, and all went back into the hotel for a late breakfast. In the dining-room, they stared at the high mountains and raised their mugs of steaming coffee. 'Adieu, Gran!' they said. 'Adieu!'

But when they came out of the hotel, blinking at the bright light, their car wasn't there. No car; no Gran; nothing.

'It's been stolen! Absolutely everything!'

Then they began to laugh.

'Gran would be laughing too,' her daughter said. 'She did love travelling.'

What's Wunce?

'ONCE,' began the teacher.

'What's wunce?' asked the little girl.

'Once,' repeated the teacher.

'Can you eat it?'

'Listen!' said the teacher. 'Once upon . . .'

'What's a pon?' asked the little girl.

'Upon,' repeated the teacher.

'Can you play with it?'

'Listen!' said the teacher. 'Once upon . . . a time.'

'A-time,' said the little girl. 'B-time. C-time. Words are so strange.'

The Spirit-Wife

THEY LIVED in the middle of the forest, seven days from the village. He hunted, she cooked; she made and mended their clothes, he gathered wood. How happy they were together! But at the beginning of winter, she turned pale and died.

The husband missed his wife so badly that after a while, he made a doll the same size and shape she had been. He made her out of wood and feathers and leaves and plaited grasses and dressed her in his wife's clothes, and set her beside the fire.

One day, when he returned after hunting, the man found his fire alight and a slab of shining red venison laid out on the hearth. Who could have left it there?

And the next day, he saw through the trees a woman, and she slipped into the hut just ahead of him.

When the man walked in, he found his own wife sitting beside the blazing fire, with stars of snow still in her hair.

'The Great Spirit can see how sad you are,' she said, 'and he has sent me back to you. I can stay with you here on one condition. You must not touch me until we have seen the people in the village.'

Husband and wife, they lived in the middle of the forest. All that snowy winter he hunted, she cooked; she made and mended their clothes, he gathered wood. And they were happy, and unhappy.

When it was nearly spring, the man said, 'How hard this winter has been! Let us walk back to the village now; and in seven days we will see all the people. Then you will be healed and I can touch you.'

By day they walked through the forest, and at night they spread out their skins to sleep. On the sixth night the man looked at his wife and his heart quickened and he reached out towards her.

'It is too soon,' said his wife.

But the man took his wife into his arms; and his wife, she turned into wood and feathers and leaves and plaited grasses.

Then the man got up and ran all the way to the village.

All the village people listened, but they didn't believe him.

'See for yourselves,' he told them.

She was still there, lying on the skin. Just a doll. And two pairs of footsteps, a woman's and a man's, led out of the forest and across the wet snow, right up to the place where the doll lay.

Me Again

FIRST HE PEERED over the peeling white courtyard door. Then he came through it and across the gravel, and sat down beside me on the wooden bench.

'Me again,' he said.

'So I see,' I replied. He was wearing a crisp, white shirt and rather baggy, old-fashioned grey shorts, and looked as pale as apple blossom.

'I mean,' said the boy, 'do you believe in ghosts? Really.'

'You asked me that before,' I said.

'And you said "yes but no" and "I'm not sure" and "it depends".'

'Well, have you ever seen this yard in moonlight?' I asked him.

The boy nodded. His hair was dark as old oak and shining, the same as mine before it turned grey.

'Roses glimmering, gravel shining,' I said. 'It looks ghostly all right.'

'I don't mean that.'

'And then people sometimes pretend to be ghosts,' I said. 'Especially at Hallowe'en. Kids chalk their faces and dress up, or drape sheets over their heads, and moan and groan.'

94

'I don't mean that, either,' said the boy. 'I mean real ghosts.'

'Last time you came,' I said, 'you told me there was a hidden nest up there, under the eaves. But when I looked, it wasn't there.'

'So?'

'But there used to be,' I said. 'I remember and you're right. There used to be. And then you led me into the gloomy, cobwebby old garage. You asked me where our boat was. And it's true, I did keep my boat there nearly fifty years ago.'

'Nearly fifty years,' echoed the boy.

'I saw the way you came through the door,' I said. 'Right through it. And I know who you are. Yes, I do believe in ghosts.'

Then, he began to fade. He always does. He was an imprint on the warm air. No more than a voice at my right ear, laughing and saying: 'Here! Behind you! Now! In front of you! Still in front of you!'

Acknowledgements

Some of these stories are original. Others are based (and in many cases very loosely based) on traditional tales to be found in *African Folktales* selected and retold by Roger D. Abrahams (New York, 1983) and the same editor's *Afro-American Folktales* (New York, 1985); *Burmese Monks' Tales* translated by Htin Aung (Calcutta, 1966); *A Dictionary of British Folk-Tales* edited by Katharine M. Briggs (London, 1970–1); *The Vanishing Hitchhiker* by Jan Harold Brunvand (London, 1981); *Arab Folktales* translated by Inea Bushnaq (New York, 1986); *Ijapa the Tortoise and Other Nigerian Tales* by Harold Courlander (New York, 1968); Charles Downing's *Armenian Folk-tales and Legends* (London, 1972) and the same author's *Russian Tales and Legends* (London, 1956); *American Indian Myths and Legends* selected and edited by Richard Erdoes and Alfonso Ortiz (New York, 1984); *Folk-Lore, III* (London, 1892); *Hindoo Fairy Legends* collected from oral tradition by Mary Frere (London, 1881); *Irish Folktales* by Henry Glassie (New York, 1985); *Indian Tales and Legends* retold by J.E.B. Gray (London, 1961); *The Complete Grimm's Fairy Tales* by Wilhelm and Jacob Grimm (New York, 1944); *Popular Romances of the West of England* by Robert Hunt (London, 1865); *Notes on the Folklore of the Northern Counties of England and the Borders* by William Henderson (London, 1866); *The Yellow Fairy Book* edited by Andrew Lang (London, 1894); *Folktales of Israel* by Dov Noy (Chicago, 1963); *Folktales of Mexico* by Americo Paredes (Chicago, 1970); *Chinese Fairy Tales and Fantasies* translated and edited by Moss Roberts (New York, 1979); *A Treasury of Mexican Folkways* by Frances Toor (New York, 1947); *Japanese Tales* edited and translated by Royall Tyler (New York, 1987); *A Treasury of Turkish Folktales for Children* retold by Barbara K. Walker (Hamden, Connecticut, 1988); and *Chinese Ghouls and Goblins* edited by G. Willoughby-Meade (London, 1928).

The author is grateful to Orchard Books for permission to reprint 'Mare's Eggs', 'Slam and the Ghosts', 'Boo!', 'Charger', and 'Poll' from his *British Folk Tales* (London, 1987). 'That's None of Your Business' was first published in his *Long Tom and the Dead Hand* (André Deutsch, London, 1992) and 'The Fox and the Geese' in *The Fox and the Cat: Animal Tales from Grimm* (Andersen, London, 1986).

Linda Waslien and her 1995–6 Year 6 class at College Heath Middle School, Mildenhall have offered helpful responses to some of these tales, and so have my own daughters, Eleanor and Oenone.